# CAPTAIN SKYWRITER

## AND KID WONDER

Stephen Elboz
and John Eastwood

Collins

# COLOUR JETS

| | |
|---|---|
| *Captain Skywriter and Kid Wonder* | Stephen Elboz |
| *Dad on the Run* | Sarah Garland |
| *Stinker Muggles and the Dazzle Bug* | Elizabeth Laird |
| *Under the Red Elephant* | Jan Mark |
| *Francis Fry, Private Eye* | Sam McBratney |
| *Even Stevens F.C.* | Michael Rosen |

*TO TIFF*
*For when she can read for herself*

First published in Great Britain by
HarperCollins Publishers Ltd 1995

1 3 5 7 9 10 8 6 4 2

Text © Stephen Elboz 1995
Illustrations © John Eastwood 1995

A CIP record for this title is available
from the British Library.

ISBN 0 00 675035-4

Printed in Italy

# Chapter 1

Baggem City…
  Night time…
    Crime time…

The people of Baggem City slept
peacefully in their beds, knowing that
their very own superhero,
Captain Skywriter, was at work.
Seeking out the bad guys…

Fighting crime…

But there was one person who never slept peacefully – Captain Skywriter's young granddaughter, Sophie.

She often sat by the open window all night, waiting for him to fly back.

She worried about him all the time.

Sophie worried because, after all, Captain Skywriter was getting on a bit.

In his youth he was known as the king of a crimefighters...

Now he was rather shortsighted.

He needed to wear his glasses all the time, otherwise he got things wrong.

Once he chased a boy eating a banana because he thought he saw a very small robber armed with a gun.

Hold it right there, buster!

But it's my lunch!

He also tended to mumble a lot.

He never **SHOUTED** in case his
false teeth flew out.

Captain Skywriter's tights were so
wrinkled that he was always stopping
to pull them up.

They don't wear glasses either, thought Sophie.

So, whenever Captain Skywriter chased a villain, he held up his tights with one hand and held his Skyzapper in the other.

But it was still no good. He was always out of breath before he reached the end of the street.

Nothing seemed to go right.

The villains of Baggem City started to laugh at him - first behind his back, then to his face.

Oops! Silly me. That must have been the ejector-button.

Never mind, Grandpa. Come and sit down. Try again tomorrow.

Hee hee hee hee hee!

13

At City Hall, Police Chief McGrabbem shook his head in despair.

## *Chapter 2*

Soon the day arrived when
Captain Skywriter hung up his winged
boots for the last time.

He put on a smart
jacket and tie.

Leaving the Skymobile in the Skycave
he caught a bus to City Hall.

Police Chief McGrabbem shook the Captain's hand, gave him a golden clock and made a very long speech.

17

Even Captain Skywriter's deadly enemy, the Slippery Shadow, sent a present.

It was a box of exploding eggs.

Luckily they exploded in time to end Police Chief McGrabbem's speech.

19

With yolk dripping off his nose and feeling more than a little sad, Captain Skywriter went off to live at Haddit House, Home for Retired Superheroes.

"It looks quite nice here," said Sophie, "with all the flowers and things."

Not as fun as leaping tall buildings with a single bound.

HADDIT HOUSE

Captain Skywriter nodded his head miserably. It looked pretty dull to him.

## Chapter 3

**Meanwhile...**

Back in the heart of Baggem City, the villains came crawling from their hideouts.

With no Captain Skywriter to **ZAP!** **POW!** or **BIFF!** them,

crime grew and **grew** and **grew**.

'WANTED' posters were stolen from the police noticeboard.

POLICE NOTICE

WA
REWA

SLIPPERY SHADOW

CRIME FIGHTING
ANOTHER LONG TALK
BY POLICE CHIEF
McGRABBEM
(BRING A PACKED LUNCH)

HAVE YOU SEEN
THIS DUCK?

DO NOT
TOUCH AS IT MAY
EXPLODE

LOST

E CAT ANSWERS
THE NAME
OF 'TIGER'

FOUND

LEFT SHOE SIZE 10
IS IT YOURS?

STOLEN

SARAH MAY DOOLEY'S
PIGGY BANK

REMOVAL
OF POSTERS FROM
THIS BOARD IS
STRICTLY
FORBIDDEN

The blankets were whipped off
Police Chief McGrabbem's bed,
from right under his nose.

Bit cold tonight, dear.

And, in the library,
printed letters were
stolen off th_ pag_s
of b__ks…

Soon the cry went up all over
Baggem City –

The job was advertised in the
newspaper –

# THE BAGGEM GLOBE

## WANTED – SUPERHERO

Must be kind to animals and willing to
work nights. No previous experience
necessary, but ability to fly would
be useful…

Many people applied for the job, but none of them were good enough to replace brave old Captain Skywriter.

27

# Chapter 4

It was then that Sophie had an idea!

I know! I'll be the next superhero.

"You?" said Captain Skywriter, smiling to himself.

"A girl?" exclaimed Police Chief McGrabbem down at City Hall.

**IT'S A GIRL!!**

**Superhero's job given to a kid.** "It'll all end in tears," predicts our crime reporter.

How the Shadow and his gang would laugh when they read it, thought the Chief.

Baby-face Brewster would laugh so much that he'd wet his nappy!

O.K. Whose turn is it to change Baby-face?

Not mine!

Sophie's Grandpa put a kind arm around her shoulder.

It's a sweet idea, child, but Sophie's no name for a superhero.

"It's too soft and fluffy."

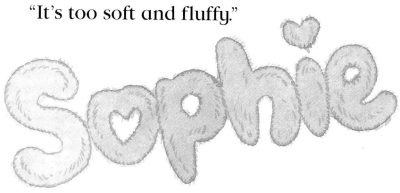

"It sounds as if it's been washed in soap."

"It sounds as if it's fresh out of a packet."

"It sounds… well… it sounds much too <u>nice</u>."

"I've thought of that," grinned Sophie. "From this moment on my name will be…

# "KID WONDER!"

"Hmm," said Captain Skywriter. "But Soph– I mean, Kid Wonder, you have to look like a real superhero, too."

"Oh, I've thought of all that," said Kid Wonder, grinning still wider. And she dashed off to change in the nearest telephone box.

When Sophie finally appeared, Captain Skywriter tried not to laugh.

33

"All I need now," said Kid Wonder, "is to learn how to fly."

Will you teach me, Grandpa? Oh, and…

…tell me what all the switches do in the Skymobile…

…and how to bend iron girders into knots.

And will you teach me how to see through walls…

…and crush stones into dust using only my bare hands?

"I can see that I shall have to," laughed Captain Skywriter.

Lessons began at once. Soon all the
retired superheroes at Haddit House
were lending a hand.

Sophie learnt quickly and, within
days, the world's newest crimefighter
was ready to take to the streets.

# Chapter 5

## *Meanwhile...*

Back in Baggem City, the Slippery Shadow called a meeting in his secret headquarters.

He was planning his latest, most daring crime. He was going to *steal time!*

Without any way of measuring time, nobody in Baggem City would know when to catch a bus...

...or have dinner...

...or go to bed.

There would be
no more
birthdays,
Christmases or
summer
holidays...

...unless, of course,
you paid the Slippery
Shadow a great deal
of money to find out
when they were.

The plan
was simple
but quite,
quite brilliant.

The Slippery Shadow's gang knew what to do.

Baby-face Brewster and Squeaky Malloy were going to nab the great clock in the tower of City Hall.

Fingers O'Brien was going to clean out the clock maker's shop.

And the Slippery Shadow himself was going to sneak the Teddy Ticker watch off the wrist of Sarah May Dooley while she slept in her bed. (Even though she'd only just had it for her birthday.)

The gang laughed at how easy it all was – but the final, most daring crime was yet to come…

## Chapter 6

The night was dark and still.

At Haddit House, Home for Retired Superheroes, not a light was to be seen, not a sound to be heard... Until...

...what was that?

It was a window slowly creaking open.

One by one,

the Slippery Shadow gang…

… **crept**

through the opening.

The gang stood still, their eyes glittering like well-sucked gobstoppers.

They carried sacks bulging with wristwatches, clocks and calendars with photographs of cute puppies.

"Shhh!" hissed the Slippery Shadow again.

The Slippery Shadow pointed at the
mantelpiece with a shaky finger.

"No! No! No!" squawked the Shadow. "Look, you fools! It's not just any old clock!"

PRESENTED TO
**CAPTAIN SKYWRITER**
ON HIS RETIREMENT
BY
THE GRATEFUL PEOPLE
OF BAGGEM CITY

"What a prize," gloated the Slippery Shadow, and he glared at his gang until they all nodded madly in agreement.

As they went on madly nodding (like Sarah May Dooley's Teddy Ticker watch), the Slippery Shadow reached out his hand and picked up the clock.

There was a soft CHINK, then the tiniest CLICK, then the smallest CLINK, and finally...

CUCK-OO!

Captain Skywriter woke up at once.

The Slippery Shadow cracked a smile at the sight of their old enemy blinking sleepily at them over the bed covers. (Especially when he saw his false teeth in a glass of water.)

"So aren't you going to **ZAP!** us?" laughed Fingers O'Brien.

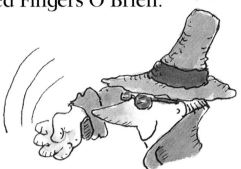

"Aren't you going to **POW!** us?" giggled Baby-face Brewster.

"Aren't you going to **BIFF!** us?" squeaked Squeaky Malloy.

"Be careful, boys," roared the Slippery Shadow. "Captain Skywriter might beat us up with his pension book."

Things looked black for the retired superhero.

# Chapter 7

The gang was so busy laughing that no one noticed Captain Skywriter press a secret button by the side of his bed.

SECRET BUTTON

In Kid Wonder's Control Centre
(well, the kitchen), a red light on the
fridge door started flashing urgently.

She ran to the nearest telephone box. (Why couldn't she just use her bedroom?)

**She arrived just in time!**

Hold it right there, you no good nicker of tickers and taker of tockers — and you can leave my Grandpa alone too.

The Slippery Shadow grinned and
looked his most dastardly.
"Don't mind her, boys. After all, she's
only a girl. A very *small* girl at that."

Before the gang could recover, Kid Wonder whipped off the cord from her Grandpa's dressing gown and flew into action.

# Chapter 8

*Next day...*

# THE BAGGEM GLOBE

# A WINNING TEAM!

## Clock thief expected to do time

Sophie just smiled.

Baggem City…
    Night time…
        Crime time…

The people of Baggem City
sleep peacefully in
their beds…

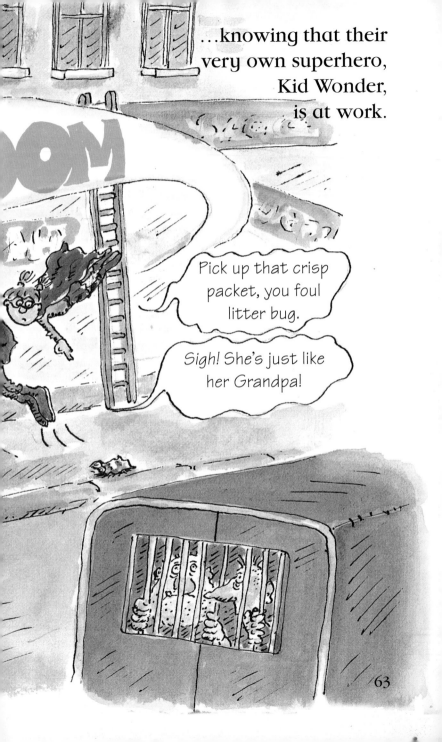

And, because superheroes don't always have time for themselves, Kid Wonder's Grandpa tends to worry more than he should.